TEAM HERO

LAIR OF THE FIRE LIZARD

ADAM BLADE

ORCHARD

SPECIAL BUMPER BOOK

MEET TEAM HERO...

JACK

POWER: Super-strength
LIKES: Ventura City FC
DISLIKES: Bullies

RUBY

POWER: Fire Vision
LIKES: Comic Books
DISLIKES: Small Spaces

DANNY

POWER: Super-hearing
LIKES: Pizza
DISLIKES: Thunder

...AND THEIR GREATEST ENEMY

GENERAL GORE

POWER: Brilliant Warrior

LIKES: Carnage

DISLIKES: Unfaithful Minions

CONTENTS

STORY 1

*"To anyone from Hero Academy
listening, I don't know where I am
and I probably don't have long.
But if you get this transmission,
do not try to rescue me."*

Ms Steel paused, taking shallow
breaths as another spasm of agony
tore through her leg. Smarm's
shadow blaster had found its target
during the battle in Noxx. The wound
was only getting worse.

*"I repeat, you must not come
here. Danger worse than
anything we have faced lurks in
waiting."*

She heard a crackle in her ear and
realised that her Oracle, Kite, must
have been damaged too. The message
might not even transmit.

She sagged back where she lay.

It was cold and dark, but she tried to fight the tides of fear threatening to overcome her. There were sounds, shuffling closer.

Through the darkness, her enemies were coming.

CHAPTER 1

A MISSING FRIEND

JACK JUMPED back as a geyser spurted from the ground only ten metres from where he was walking. A jet of steaming water arced into the air, then cascaded down, splashing the trousers of Jack's silver snowsuit.

"This place is amazing!" said Ruby, her amber eyes shining.

"As long as you don't get boiled alive," said Jack, eyeing the bare rocky ground.

"I'll listen out for anything else that might cook us," said Danny, tucking his straight black hair behind his bat-like ears.

All around them, among the stunted trees and boulders, pools of turquoise water glistened. The strangest thing was how icy the air was, even though they were practically walking on a volcano. But then, they were in the Arctic Circle.

"Hawk, switch to infrared vision," Jack said.

"Wonderful idea!" replied the Oracle in his ear. "The landscape will be even more impressive in thermal vision."

A visor extended from the earpiece over one of Jack's eyes. The terrain showed in shades of blue and white, with hotspots of orange, yellow and red.

If only we were here just to enjoy the view, Jack thought.

But they were on an important Team Hero mission.

The recent battle in Noxx had been a success, in some ways. Jack and his friends had defeated General Gore, and prevented his armies from coming to the earth's surface to spread their reign of terror and shadow. But they had paid a high price. During the duel between Jack and Gore, Hero Academy teacher Ms Steel had been wounded by Smarm, the general's sorcerer. She'd teleported herself away, but she'd never turned up at the school. She was officially Missing in Action. The longer that was the case, the slimmer the odds of her survival became.

Though they had won the battle, Professor Rufus said the war against the forces of darkness wasn't over. General Gore might have been vanquished, but the forces of Noxx were vast. They could regroup and find a new leader, and would never stop seeking revenge on the human world. A week had passed, and many of the faculty were stationed in the ruins of Noxx, checking there was no further threat. But several other Team Hero squads had been dispatched around the globe to monitor other locations where the Noxxians might plan to break through — sinkholes, caves, deep ravines, volcanoes. Jack and his team had been sent north. Their specially adapted bodysuits kept out the worst of the arctic winds. But in Jack's heart, the cold dread remained.

If Ms Steel is dead, I'll never forgive myself. I should have protected her from Smarm.

Jack quickened his pace, peering ahead. This area was home to a deep fissure, well below sea level, and spanning several kilometres. He and his friends had been tasked with the job of searching it for any signs of Noxxian technology, using their personal Oracles. It was painstaking work. They couldn't afford to miss anything. The fate of the world depended on it.

"Do you really think the Noxxians are coming back?" asked Danny, as they trudged up a rocky slope.

"I hope not," said Ruby. Jack could see only a small patch of her dark skin behind the furred hood she wore. Like her uniform at the academy, her silver bodysuit had yellow tabs on the shoulders, showing her school house. "It's probably just a precaution."

At the brow of the hill, Jack bristled. Something approached through the falling snow — a giant creature with eight legs, each one thumping into the rock and ice, two eyes glowing like small suns. They focused their glare on Jack and his friends as the metal beast stamped towards them.

Then, with a hydraulic hiss, the legs folded on themselves, and the spider's car-sized body lowered. A hatch opened, and a Team Hero unit clambered out, all dressed in silver suits with green shoulder pads. Though their faces were covered too, Jack recognised their leader at

once, just from the arrogant way
he strutted forward. As they came
together, the boy lowered his face-
scarf. Olly.

"Well, look who it is!" Olly said. He put his hand to his ear, eyes suddenly going wide. "Wait, guys!" he called to the others. "My Oracle is picking something up." He pointed at Jack. "Oh, that's it — it's picking up a major loser!"

The others burst out laughing.

"Have you found anything?" asked Jack, ignoring the taunts.

The spider was designed for climbing. Its eight legs could anchor it on slopes where no other vehicle would even stand a chance. Olly's team had been handling the eastern end of the trench, and now Jack's were taking over to work along the western end.

"Nope," said Olly. "This is such a waste of time."

"We have to be thorough," said Ruby. "If we miss something—"

"You really think General Gore would dare?" said Olly. "I'd like to see him try! I'd take him on single-handed. I'd—"

"Centipede soldier!" cried Danny, pointing.

Olly leapt into air with a yelp and hovered there, hands over his head.

Everyone started laughing, including his own team.

"I was just kidding," said Danny.

Olly went bright red and flew over to Jack, landing on the ground. "By the way, that spider is a heap of junk," he sneered. "I do hope it doesn't give up on you. We're a long way from home. If you fall, they'll probably just leave you down there."

He and the green team stalked off.

The other side of the hill, the ground opened up in a huge crevasse like a dark scar in the wintry landscape. Jack peered over the edge but couldn't see the bottom.

"I guess that's where we're headed," he said.

They walked across to the spider rover, and climbed in. Olly hadn't been lying about it being a bit worse for wear. The thing must have been left outside for too long, because patches of rust covered its metal skin, and when Jack started it up, the joints screeched horribly. He found the wipers and they cleared a layer of grit and snow from the viewing shield.

Jack asked Hawk to bring up a diagram of the rover's controls on his visor. After flying a Noxxian portal shuttle out of the collapsing underground realm, Jack didn't think this thing could be too difficult. He

checked the diagram then pushed
a lever forward, guiding the metal
spider towards the crevasse in
lumbering steps. He stopped the
machine at the edge. "Hold tight," he
said, easing the control stick forward.

Two of the robotic legs braced against the crevasse's far wall, as the spider's body tilted forward. Jack's heart rattled against his ribcage. If the machine failed now, it was a long, long drop.

Ruby turned on the spider's eyelamps. Beams of light flooded the crevasse, but all Jack saw was bare rock descending deep into the ground. "Much better," Ruby said, though her voice sounded shaky.

"It's over four thousand metres down to the base," said Danny, reading off measurements from the mapping system.

Jack guided the spider down the crevasse. Its sharp feet reached out and stabbed into the rock below, while the other legs held its weight.

The chasm was silent. Jack started to think that Olly might be right ...

"I'm picking up a signal," said Hawk. "It's a recorded message."

"Play it," said Jack.

There was the hiss of static as Hawk synched with Ruby and Danny's Oracles, then Jack heard a voice he knew well.

Ms Steel's.

"To anyone from the Hero Academy listening, I don't know where I am and I probably don't have long. If you get this transmission ..."

The signal broke up into a crackle.

Jack stared at the others. "Ms Steel is down here! And she sounds hurt!"

CHAPTER 2

INTO THE DEEP

RUBY PRESSED her Oracle to her ear.
"Kestrel, open a line of communication.
Ms Steel? Ms Steel, can you hear me?"

The message replayed.

"*To anyone from the Hero Academy
listening, I don't know where I am and
I probably don't have long. If you get
this transmission ...*"

31

"The message was sent from her Oracle," said Hawk. "It is set to play on repeat."

"But she's close, right?" said Jack.

"I detect no signs of life," said Hawk.

Jack swallowed. "You mean she's ..." He couldn't bring himself to finish the sentence.

"Quite possibly," said Hawk. "But there are other potential explanations. The volcanic activity and magnetic interference of the North Pole may be affecting my sensors."

Jack ordered Hawk to open a channel to Chancellor Rex, their headmaster. He was overseeing the search in Noxx itself. A grainy image of a tall, straight-backed man with grey hair and a silver bodysuit appeared on Jack's visor. Behind him Jack saw the craggy landscape of Noxx, with looming stalagmites and the orange glow of the lava falls.

"Report, Jack," he said.

"Sir, we've found a message from Ms Steel," he said.

"Sending across now," said Hawk. For a few seconds, the chancellor listened to the message in his Oracle, then his brow creased in a frown.

"Hang back for now, team."

"What?" asked Jack. "She might be

injured. We need to rescue—"

Rex shook his head firmly.
"Negative. I can't risk you three
without first knowing what you're
dealing with. Wait for backup."

"But how long will that take?"
asked Ruby.

Chancellor Rex's image flickered,
and they couldn't hear his voice. Then
he vanished.

"It's the magnetic interference,"
said Danny.

Jack thumped the rover's
dashboard with a scaled fist, harder
than he intended — his superstrong
hand left a dent.

Ruby shook her head. "Reinforcements won't be here for hours, and it sounded from her message like Ms Steel doesn't have that long."

"We can't leave her trapped down there," said Danny, his face taking on a haunted look. He knew what it was like being held captive alone, deep underground. After Danny had been poisoned by shadow, he'd been imprisoned in Noxx by Skulgar, Gore's jailer. The memory gave Jack an idea.

"Hawk, can you track Ms Steel's Oracle like you did with Danny's in Noxx?"

"Kite's location signal is too weak," said Hawk. "But I can give you the last known coordinates."

"I say we go after her now," said Jack, hands back on the controls. "You both with me?"

Ruby nodded firmly.

"What about Olly and his team?" asked Danny. "Do you think we should get them too?"

"The spider only has enough room for one team," said Jack. "And we can't waste time."

"Sounds like it's Team Hero to the rescue!" said Ruby.

Jack pulled and pushed the control

levers, and the spider descended, clanking, into darkness. It was a bumpy ride as the robot reached and latched on to the ledge and cracks in the crevasse walls. Jack's breath quickened. *One slip and we're all dead.*

At his side, Danny was checking the bolts for his crossbow. He had an assortment, designed for different functions, whether explosive or shadow-seeking, or sonic detonating. Ruby spun her mirrored shield on her arm. The silver spines around the edge glittered.

The rover lurched suddenly with a

grinding sound as two of the spider's legs lost purchase on the wall. Panic lanced through Jack's gut. Danny cried out and Ruby's eyes flashed red.

"We're falling!" she cried.

Jack's hands tightened on the controls, slamming the legs into the rock with a screech of metal. Sparks scored the air on either side of the crevasse. But they were falling too fast, and Jack knew it.

Hawk's voice spoke calmly into Jack's ear.

"900 metres to impact …"

Jack felt his body thrown against the belt as the spider slammed into a

ledge, tipping them over and sending
them into a spin.

"800 metres to impact."

The glass viewing screen exploded
into fragments as they careened
against the side of the crevasse. Held
into his seat by a safety belt, Jack

hung upside down.

"700 metres. 600 metres."

The spider righted itself, but it was plummeting faster than ever. The black walls were a blur.

"500 metres. 400 metres."

"We need to do something!" Ruby shouted desperately.

"That would be wise," said Hawk. "300 metres."

Jack knew he risked being thrown from the cockpit, but, gripping his seat with one scaled hand, he unclipped his seat belt. He crouched on the seat, holding himself steady, and drew Blaze, his sunsteel blade.

"Grab onto me!" he cried. His hands, he noticed, had already begun to glow gold. His power surged through them by instinct alone.

"200 metres."

"Do what?" yelled Danny.

"Now!" roared Jack. He jumped through the space where the windshield had been.

"100 metres."

He felt his friends' arms wrap around his legs. Using all his super strength, he jammed the sword into the crevasse wall. The blade sank into the rock, slowing him instantly and throwing showers of sparks into the

darkness. The spider fell away below, smashing into the sides of the chasm. Jack's joints screamed with pain as he held the weight of himself and his friends. A second later the rover hit the bottom of the crevasse with a deafening crash. Orange flames lit up the crevasse floor.

Jack breathed a huge sigh, grinning down at his friends. "There's a ledge below you."

Ruby and Danny jumped down onto the narrow shelf of rock. Hands glowing, Jack tugged the sword from the wall and dropped next to them.

"You saved our lives," said Ruby, slapping him on the back.

Danny looked too shocked to speak, mouth opening and closing. "Let's not do that again," he croaked eventually.

They were only thirty metres or so above the bottom of the chasm, which flickered in the orange glow of the burning spider bot.

Professor Rufus is not going to be happy.

There were plenty of handholds to pick their way down. Still, by the time Jack reached the bottom of the crevasse, his chest was heaving. He noticed that his breath no longer clouded in front of him.

It's warm down here.

"Hawk, which way did Kite go?"
he asked.

"To your left," said the Oracle.

Jack noticed a dark passage in that
direction, burrowing into the side
of the crevasse. With a nod to the
others, Jack hurried forward, entering
the dark opening. Ruby used the fire-
beams from her eyes to light up the
way. After a hundred metres, the
passage widened into a vast cavern.

Here, they didn't need Ruby's light
anymore, because the walls were
covered in glowing fungus — strange

swollen growths, some bigger than Jack himself, clinging to the rock. Their light reflected off underground pools of water so blue and still they were like mirrors of a cloudless summer sky. They moved on, coming across a tall, bone-white tree.

"Impossible," said Ruby. "There's no light down here. No soil."

The tree jutted up from the ground like an elegant hand clutching at the air. And there were more as they went on — a whole forest.

"This place is beautiful," muttered Danny, awestruck.

Jack nodded, but he gripped Blaze's

hilt, remembering the fear in Ms
Steel's voice. She had been scared

Picking their way between the trees,
Jack sucked in a breath. In the gloom,
a few kilometres away, a mountain
rose up hundreds of metres high.

"Wow," muttered Ruby.

Danny went still. "I can hear
something."

Jack looked at him, pulse thumping
in his throat. "Ms Steel?"

"I don't know. Follow me."

Danny led them off on a path
between two pools, and soon even
Jack could hear something — a
scuttling and hissing and thumping.

They came to a clearing and saw two creatures play-fighting on the ground. Jack gawped. He'd never seen anything like them. They were lizards, each about the size of a dog, and made out of rock. Flames licked gently over their bodies.

"Pretty cute," said Ruby.

Jack let his blade drop. "Yeah, they don't seem too bad."

"Er ... what about that one?" said Danny, pointing behind them.

Jack turned and saw a similar creature, but about the size of a pony, striding across the ground towards them, trailing ash in its wake.

"Maybe it's the mummy," said Ruby.

The larger lizard stopped. A blast
of fire spurted from its black jaws.
Ruby raised her shield. Danny and
Jack jumped behind her. But the fire
stopped well short, though Jack still
felt the searing heat bathe his face.

"Maybe we've outstayed our welcome," he said.

The words had only just left his mouth, when half a dozen more flame lizards stalked over.

We're being surrounded.

"Can you warn them off?" Danny asked Ruby nervously.

Ruby touched her temple. Her eyes glowed and a jet of flame shot out at one of the larger creatures. But halfway to the lizard, the fire fizzled out, turning to smoke. Ruby shot another beam but again it died quickly. Ruby frowned. "I don't know what's wrong."

The largest lizard reared back, with a roar. Shaking its head from side to side, it advanced towards Jack and his friends. He heard snorts and jaws clacking from behind him and glanced over to see the entire pack of creatures closing in around them.

The lizards opened their mouths, revealing shards of stone teeth. Fire swirled in their throats.

"I think you may have angered them," said Hawk.

"Tell me something I don't know," Jack replied.

CHAPTER 3

RUINS OF NOXX

TWO CREATURES lunged for Jack's legs, while the largest blew out a stream of fire. Jack kicked away the creatures, as Ruby dived in front of the fire stream, deflecting it with her mirror shield.

"OK, maybe they're not so cute!" she cried above the noise.

"This way!" shouted Danny, sprinting through a gap between two of the flame lizards.

Jack and Ruby followed him, jumping over a smaller creature, which snapped at their ankles. Jack felt a blast of flames licking at his back. The three friends zigzagged out of range, skirting the channels of turquoise water flowing between the pale trees, and leaping over the smaller pools. In some places the trees were packed tight together, and the branches whipped Jack's skin.

After a few minutes, Ruby slowed down. "I think we've lost them."

"I don't get it," Danny panted as he leaned against a tree. "I should have heard all those creature approaching. But my ears don't seem as sharp as normal."

"I know what you mean," replied Ruby. "My eyes somehow don't feel as powerful, either."

They both looked at Jack. His hands felt normal. To test this, he found a fallen tree and slid his hands under the dead bark. He hoisted the trunk above his head, easily.

"All right, show-off," said Danny. "I don't want to wait around for those weird flame lizards — especially when

my powers aren't working properly."
He touched his earpiece. "Owl, tell us
which way to go."

"Towards the mountain," replied the
Oracle, speaking through Hawk.

They set off once more, pushing
through the white tree branches and

leaping over the glimmering pools.
Soon Jack started to notice that
the trunks of the trees were stained
dark in places, and some of the
branches drooped.

*It's like they've been rotted by a
disease,* thought Jack.

They reached a stream about two
metres across. Danny was about to
leap over, when Ruby grabbed his arm.

"Wait!" she said, pointing downwards.

Jack saw threads of darker water
spreading through the glistening
stream. They writhed and twisted in a
way that was all too familiar. "Oh, no,"
said Jack.

"Noxxian shadow," Danny whispered, staring into the water with fearful eyes. The foul darkness turned anything it touched evil.

Jack's stomach twisted with dread. *What if Ms Steel has come into contact with it? We might already be too late to save her.*

They walked along the bank of the stream a little way, and soon the water cleared. They waded through a narrower point and continued towards the mountain. But it wasn't long until they saw more evidence of disease. The trees withered, the ground around them softer and mulchy. And in some places the pools of water were pure black, as if ruined by tar. Jack didn't like it at all. It looked like a fire had swept through the underground realm. But Jack knew it must be the shadow that was causing the decay. And it seemed to be spreading from the mountain itself.

As the dead forest thinned around them, Jack saw that the top of the mountain's peak was covered in pale grass, but its base was black and dead.

"I don't like this place," said Ruby.

"It wouldn't be my choice for a holiday either," said Jack. "Hawk, where now?"

"Straight ahead," replied the Oracle. "Four hundred metres."

"We're almost there," said Jack. He began to shout. "Ms Steel!"

Breaking into a run, he dodged through the blackened trees. He emerged into a clearing. "Ms Ste—" He broke off, seeing some sort of raised black structure ahead, not far from the base of the mountain. It was a building, its dark stone walls merging with the dead landscape. The nearer they got, the larger it loomed.

"Do you think Ms Steel is in that?" asked Danny quietly. "I can't tell. It's like I'm hearing underwater."

"Only one way to find out," said Ruby. She hurried up to a set of huge stone stairs that led up into a doorway. The steps were each higher than Jack's waist, and crumbling in places. Jack used his hands to vault up three stairs in one go.

"Why are they so big?" Danny panted as he pulled himself up the first. Jack reached down to lend the others a hand.

He knew Ms Steel could be close, but a creeping dread in the pit of his stomach stopped Jack from calling out. He climbed the rest of the steps, then walked through the doorway

at the top. He gasped. The ground
ahead had been dug away, so he was
standing on the lip of a vast basin.
In the middle of the dip lay the ruins
of what must have once been an
enormous temple complex. The stubs
of columns were dotted at intervals.

Others had collapsed sideways or into
one another. The remains of statues
— some headless or missing limbs —
stood among them on plinths. Jack's
skin crawled as he saw they weren't
sculptures of men and women, but
terrifying hybrid creatures — reptile

men, insects with human faces, giant bats, skeletons. Many clutched horrible weapons.

"They're Noxxian creatures," Jack said pointing them out to the others, who'd reached the top of the stairs.

"That disease killing all the trees is definitely shadow, then," said Danny. "It explains why our powers are weakened too."

"And why yours aren't," added Ruby. "The Chosen One is immune to the shadow's touch."

Jack nodded grimly. "Come on."

They descended more steps into the depths of the ancient temple. In the centre, a single soaring obelisk remained. The needle of black rock towered ten metres high. Right at the top of it, Jack could see the engraving of a sun...

The black sun of Noxx, spilling lashes of shadow.

"The symbol of General Gore," said Danny, his crossbow trembling a little.

"This place is clearly an outpost of some sort," said Ruby.

Jack swallowed thickly. "Yep," he said. "And we've walked right into the middle of it."

CHAPTER 4

FLAME LIZARD

JACK DREW Blaze, and its keen edge shimmered brightly, reacting to the shadow.

"It looks abandoned," said Ruby, amber eyes travelling over the broken walls and ancient statues.

Jack kept his eyes peeled. *I hope she's right ...* "Let's be on our guard," he said. "Once we've found Ms Steel, we can get back to the surface and let the others know what we've discovered."

Beyond the huge obelisk, they found a statue on its side. Even covered in rubble, Jack knew it was of General Gore. He was wearing his thick plated armour, his helmet covering most of his face. The sculpted folds of his cloak were chipped in places. His arm, clutching the Shadow Sword, lay detached on the ground beside a plinth. A single foot was still stuck to the plinth's base.

"Something's written there," said Ruby, leaning close to the plinth. Jack squinted, but the markings were not letters he understood. "Kestrel, can you translate?" Ruby asked. She frowned. "She says it will take time."

Then Jack heard another sound, and it sounded like laughter on the wind — the sickening, hateful laughter of General Gore. Jack spun around, but neither of the others seemed to have noticed. He felt a shiver pass down his spine.

"Owl says Kite is this way," Danny said, leading Jack and Ruby past Gore's shattered statue and up the steps at the other side of the sunken temple.

Looking back, Jack saw new swirls of shadow licking around the ruins. He didn't think they'd been there before, but he couldn't be sure.

A boulder field strewn with rubble separated them from the base of the mountain. Jack guessed this was where the Noxxians had mined the stone to build the temple.

"Unable to translate the inscription," said Kestrel's voice in Jack's ear, synced with Hawk. "Give me some more time."

"I don't understand," said Danny. "According to Owl, we should be right on top of where Kite's signal was."

"Ms Steel!" called Ruby. "Can you hear us?"

As they hopped from one boulder to the next, Jack's eyes caught a metallic flash below, to his right. He sheathed Blaze, jumped down to the pebbly floor and rushed over to where a smashed earpiece lay, trailing wires. Jack's heart sank.

It was the remains of Ms Steel's Oracle, Kite.

Ruby's face fell. "What ... what does it mean?"

Jack shook his head. "I don't know. But Ms Steel would never have taken out her Oracle willingly." As Jack

spoke, he noticed marks in the rock
nearby — scratch marks. They were
spaced far apart, made by something
huge. Jack pointed at them. "I think
something might have attacked her."

Ruby's eyes flashed. "We need to
find her! But she could be anywhere."

"Owl?" Danny asked. "Can you get any data from Kite?"

As Owl went to work, Jack cast worried glances around. Among all these huge boulders, they couldn't see any enemies coming. Whatever had attacked Ms Steel might be right around the corner and they wouldn't know until it was too late.

"Owl has managed to upload the last message Ms Steel recorded to Kite," said Hawk.

After a crackle of static, Jack heard his teacher's voice clearly.

"To anyone from the Hero Academy listening, I don't know where I am and

I probably don't have long. But if you get this transmission, do not try to rescue me." There was a pause, and Jack thought he could hear Ms Steel suck in a breath. She was in pain. *"I repeat, you must not come here. Danger worse than anything we have faced lurks in wait."*

The message ended, and Jack saw the fear painted on his friends' faces.

"It wasn't a call for help after all," said Danny quietly. "It was a warning to stay away."

"We're not leaving without Ms Steel," said Jack. He still held the smashed Oracle in his hand, remembering what Professor Rufus had told him about them. "These things are made of an incredibly strong alloy," he said. "It must have taken a massive force to break it."

"Is that supposed to make me feel better?" asked Danny.

"Wait here," said Jack. He began to climb a nearby boulder – the biggest he could see. If he could get a better vantage point, it might help make sense of what had happened to Ms Steel.

As he reached the top, he surveyed the vast boulder field. The mountain rose ahead, and behind them was the

temple and the forest. Not a single
sign of life anywhere.

The boulder beneath his feet shifted a little, and he struggled to keep his balance. Was it some sort of earthquake?

Danny and Ruby were staring up at him, eyes wide with alarm. Danny levelled his crossbow.

"Jack!" Ruby shouted. "You need to get off there. Now!"

Before Jack had had time to think, the boulder moved once more. Only this time, the stone seemed to flex. Jack fell to his knees, staring in horror as more boulders nearby stirred. A line of rocks formed a ridged tail on one side, and on the

other a stubby head and snout lifting up. It was like an enormous dinosaur, but made of rock, parts of its body glowing red with heat.

"It's a flame lizard!" shouted Danny.

The head twisted back, and the

stone split apart to reveal an angry
red eye, looking straight at him.

CHAPTER 5

GORE'S SERVANT

JACK THREW himself off the creature's back. He landed hard and rolled towards his friends, already reaching for the sword at his belt.

"Did that thing eat Ms Steel?" cried Ruby, lowering her spiked shield in a defensive pose.

Danny notched a bolt on his

crossbow, pointing it at the giant rock-like creature.

The stone-scaled lizard was twice as long as a bus. As it turned, it shouldered boulders aside as if they were pebbles. Now, both raging eyes settled on Jack and his friends. It let out a series of bellows and grunts.

"I think it might be trying to talk to us," said Jack.

"Maybe it's friendly?" said Danny.

"Hawk, can you translate?" Jack asked his oracle.

"I am no expert in lizardish," said Hawk, "but I don't think it likes you."

The lizard opened its mouth,

revealing a black chasm of a throat and stone teeth the size of swords. Jack saw red flames building in the back of its throat.

"Move!" he shouted, pushing Danny and Ruby with his scaled hands. It was a light shove, but they both flew through the air, and Jack leapt the other way. A jet of fire spurted from the monster's mouth, scorching the ground where they'd been standing.

"Maybe it's not so friendly after all," said Danny.

Ruby picked herself up and touched her temple. Twin fire-beams slammed into the monster's neck, and it reared back with a roar. But the beams died quickly, and the fire didn't seem to have any effect.

Danny had loaded a glowing white bolt into his crossbow. *Liquid sunlight,* Jack realised. Professor Rufus had been working on anti-shadow weaponry for years, designed to tackle creatures from Noxx. The bolt whined through the air, exploding against the creature's ridged back in a shower of sparks.

As the smoke cleared, Jack saw that the beast was completely unscathed.

The lizard breathed a blast of glowing flame towards Danny, who

jumped clear as the boulder he'd
been standing on turned molten and
collapsed into thick lava.

"Danny!" Ruby cried.

Jack rushed forwards under the cover
of a smoke cloud, fearing the worst, but
Danny was safely on the ground.

"I don't understand," he said. "My arrows are useless."

"Maybe it's not a creature of Noxx," said Jack.

"If it's not, then how do we fight it?" asked Ruby.

"We have to stay alive first. This way." Jack zigzagged through the smoke, hiding behind a large boulder. He could hear the monster hauling itself between the strewn rocks, looking for them. *We can't hide forever*, thought Jack.

"Let's split up," he said, drawing Blaze. "Your weapons might not work, but maybe mine will."

"Basically, you think we should be bait," said Ruby.

"If you want to put it like that," said Jack, with a grin.

The boulder they were behind rocked as the lizard brushed past.

Now, mouthed Jack.

Ruby and Danny ran out. "Hey, rock features!" Danny cried.

The beast wheeled around and sent a spout of flame after Jack's friend.

"No, over here!" called Ruby. She fired her eye-beams at the lizard from the other side. It turned again, thrashing wildly.

Jack took his chance and ran full

pelt from behind. Leaping from one stony spike to the next, he scaled the boulders of the monster's tail and back until he reached its shoulders. His golden hands glowed as he swung

the flat of the blade towards the stone flesh of its head.

CLANG!

The beast hissed with pain and rage, then began to charge. Jack hung on with one hand as it smashed a path through the rocks. As they bounced along, he saw that the creature's stone flesh was scarred in many places with gouges already, and he wondered what could have caused such injuries. Looking behind, he saw his friends sprinting after them. He wasn't sure what they planned to do. He wasn't sure what he planned to do either, other than hang on for dear life.

When they reached the foot of the mountain, the lizard suddenly jammed its front claws into the ground, skidding to a halt. Jack was hurled loose, sword slipping from his hands. He somersaulted through the air, over the monster's head and crashed into the hard ground. He tumbled over and over, sharp debris cutting his arms and face. Finally he came to a stop on his back, gasping for breath and pain searing his side. He could hardly move, but through the dust he saw why the stone beast had ceased its rampage. All around the base of the mountain was a knot of thick thorny vines that towered several metres off the ground. They looked like they were made from some sort of metal, gleaming cruelly like giant barbed wire.

Jack realised at once that these were what had caused the old wounds on the beast's flanks.

Someone else had put this barrier here, but why?

"Jack, are you OK?" Ruby arrived at his side with Danny, both of their faces streaked with sweat and dirt.

Jack rolled onto his knees and stood. "I've been better," he said, picking up his sword.

The enormous fire-breathing lizard was pacing ten metres away, but not coming any closer.

"It's scared of the thorns," said Jack. "I think we're safe here."

"Not true, I'm afraid," said a voice.

They all spun around. Standing in a doorway carved into the mountain slope, half-hidden by the metal vines, was a figure Jack thought he'd never lay eyes on again.

"Bulk!" whispered Ruby.

Gore's bald henchman wore an armless tunic of scuffed leather, his pale flesh bulging from underneath, and his mouth split in a glistening, toothless leer. He carried a double-headed axe in a stubby hand, his filthy nails bitten down to the quick.

So, the Noxxians haven't abandoned this place completely, thought Jack.

"Nice to see you all again," said Bulk conversationally.

Jack pointed Blaze at him. "What is this place?" he said.

"Your grave," said Bulk. He scratched a patch of skin where his belly hung over his belt.

Danny aimed his crossbow. "Tough words, considering it's three against one," he said.

Bulk picked his nose, and stepped

further from the doorway. Ten
skeleton warriors marched out,
bodies rattling. They formed a semi-
circle in front of Jack and his friends,
and brandished scimitars made of
carved bone.

"I suppose you're looking for the
other one — the woman," said Bulk.
He sniggered. "I'm sorry to say, my
friend Smarm's got her." He gestured
backwards with the axe-head,
towards the door into the mountain.

"Hand her over!" said Ruby.

"No chance," said Bulk. His eyes
rested on something behind them. "Oh
goody — feeding time!"

Jack turned to see the pack of smaller flame lizards had caught up with them. They all swarmed towards the larger one. The clacks and grunts and bellows grew louder as the creatures talked to one another. The little ones gathered around the legs of the huge monster.

"She's their mother!" Jack exclaimed.

"That's right," said Bulk. "Tartania likes to make sure her little ones eat proper meals." He chuckled. "As you'll soon see."

Jack knew they were trapped — the skeleton soldiers ahead, and the flame lizards behind. He slowed his breathing, thinking of all the training he'd received at Hero Academy. Something Ms Steel had once said to him in battle classes swirled into his brain. *The element of surprise can defeat superior numbers.*

"You know how to play skittles?" Jack whispered to his friends, looking pointedly towards the skeleton posse.

Danny and Ruby both nodded, smiles slowly replacing the panic across their faces.

Tartania gave a rattling call, and all the smaller creatures turned their hungry gazes on the three friends.

"This is going to be fun," said Bulk.

"Now!" said Jack.

He spun on his heel and ran at
Bulk's squadron
of soldiers. Gore's
hairless minion
opened his mouth
in shock, just as
the first of Danny's
sunlight crossbow
bolts blasted a
skeleton to shadows.
Ruby's beams
cut through a
couple, while Jack
swung his sword

in a downward sweep. The skeleton exploded into bony fragments.

"Stop them!" roared Bulk.

But Jack and the others were gone already, piling through the door. Ruby came last, and slammed it closed behind them. Jack found a wooden bar and quickly slid it into place.

Fists pounded the other side, and he heard Bulk crying out. "Back, Tartania. No … Please …" Then his shouts became a wail of fear.

The friends found themselves in a dim corridor heading into darkness. Jack dreaded to think what waited for them in the heart of the mountain, but at least they'd learned from Bulk that Ms Steel was still alive, even if she was a hostage to Smarm.

"While you were playing heroes," said Hawk, "Kestrel and I translated that inscription. It was quite the job, as the language was unknown to human scholars, so we had to run a mathematical pattern detector in order to—"

"Just tell us what it said," said Jack.

"Very well. It reads as follows: *All hail to the hero, General Gore – leader of our realm. It was on this spot that the mighty one was resurrected in the year 1004. May his eternal spirit crush his enemies."*

Jack felt the blood drain from his face. At the academy, Chancellor Rex had often wondered how Gore had been brought back to life after his defeat by Team Hero a thousand years ago. Now they had the answer.

"I bet that's why Smarm and Bulk are here," said Ruby.

"What do you mean?" asked Danny, not following.

"I mean that if they brought him back once, then they can do it again," said Jack solemnly. "And it's up to us to stop them."

STORY 2

Ms Steel had never felt so weak.

She lay in a cage, the bars wreathed in coils of swirling shadow. Beyond them stretched the underground lake, with waters black as a slick of tar. This whole place was poisoned with General Gore's essence.

And if Smarm has his way, this is the place at which Gore will return.

The gaunt sorcerer was standing on the banks on the lake, chanting towards an object he held over the water — General Gore's black helmet. Ms

Steel didn't understand the strange tongue Smarm was speaking, but she understood what he was trying to do.

Summon his master.

She managed to push herself up, but when she tried to teleport, the result was the same as before. The shadow had drained her powers.

That was why it was so important to keep the rest of Team Hero away. If any of them made a rescue attempt, the shadow would sap them, just as it had drained her. All their powers would be useless.

Well, not all. But even Jack, the Chosen One, would be a fool to risk his life down here.

CHAPTER 1

STEPPING STONES

"BUT WE defeated him." Danny shook his head. "Gore is buried under the cavern in Noxx."

Jack didn't know how the general's resurrection was possible. All he knew was that it was happening.

"That has to be why the forest outside is dying and its waters are corrupted," he said. "Gore's shadow spirit must be getting stronger."

"And it explains why our powers are weakening," said Ruby.

"It's all right for some," grumbled Danny, nodding towards Jack. "One of us is immune to shadow."

"You're right," said Jack. "Maybe you two should stay here." He turned towards the depths of the mountain. "I can find Ms Steel on my own."

"No way!" said Ruby. "We're staying!" She nudged Danny. "Aren't we?"

"Sure," said Danny, grinning at Jack. "Lead the way, Chosen One."

Jack asked Hawk to switch to

night-vision, and the Oracle filtered his vision into shades of green.

The tunnel ahead was roughly hewn, musty, and leading downwards. Jack kept his eyes peeled for any sign of Noxxian troops.

The air became gradually hotter and the passage widened. The walls were green and mossy at first, then trailed with metallic vines, like the ones set around the base of the mountain.

"These aren't natural," said Ruby, peering closer at one. "Someone has put them here. Woah!" She jerked back as one of the vines snaked away from the wall and towards her.

At once, all the foliage came to life, darting like flickering tongues, searching for prey. Standing in the centre of the wide tunnel, Jack and his friends were just out of reach. Jack didn't want to think what might happen if they actually managed to snag on someone.

We'll be torn to pieces.

"Be careful," he said. "This place is filled with Gore's shadow spirit. We have to assume that everything is out to kill us."

"Not much change there, then," said Danny wryly.

As they crept between the vines, the temperature rose until it became almost unbearable.

"Hawk," said Jack. "Can you do

something about this heat?"

"A cold beverage, perhaps? I'm afraid I'm not a waiter."

"What about our suits?" said Jack.

"I can activate the heat reflective cells," said Hawk.

"Thank you!" said Jack.

Almost at once, a feeling like a refreshing breeze wafted over him. Looking down, he saw his suit was shimmering slightly, as if covered with a thin layer of water, but when he touched it, it felt normal.

His friends' suits activated the same feature. "That's better," said Danny. "Like a cool bath!"

Once they cleared the vines, Jack quickened his pace. The thought of Ms Steel in the clutches of evil Smarm made his chest tighten. He obviously wanted her for something, otherwise he would have killed her long ago.

"Uh-oh," said Ruby.

Jack stopped. Ahead, the ground fell away in a huge ravine.

Jack blinked and he heard his friends gasp beside him. A line of stones hovered at intervals over the abyss, like flying stepping stones. Some were several metres across, others much smaller.

"How is that even possible?" said
Danny. "Some of those rocks must
weigh tonnes!"

"I remember Professor Rufus
talking about places where gravity
behaves differently," said Ruby.

"I think we can use them to cross."

"You think?" said Danny.

"I hope," said Ruby.

"We don't have any other choice,"
said Jack. For a moment he found
himself wishing they had Olly with

them. With his flying ability, he might have been able to carry them across, one at a time.

Mind you, knowing Olly, he'd probably drop one of us.

Jack took a few steps back, ready to run and leap to the first stone.

"Wait!" said Ruby, shrugging off her backpack. "I took this from the spider rover." She pulled out a rope. "Hold on to it. Danny and I will hold the other end in case you fall."

Jack did as she said. "Here goes nothing," he muttered. He ran to the edge of the ravine and leapt into thin air. His feet landed neatly on the first stone, which was about the size of a table top. It wobbled a little, and a rush of cold panic swooped through his chest. But the stone held his weight. He stood up slowly, arms out for balance. He turned back to the others. "I think it's safe."

Danny came next, landing beside Jack, who grabbed his arm, steadying him. Last of all, Ruby jumped, holding onto the rope. As soon as her feet hit the stone, it began to tip. Jack planted his foot on the other side to balance it. They clung to each other until the rocking settled down.

"This could be tricky," said Danny.

The other side suddenly looked a long way off.

The next nearest stone was much smaller. It was barely a metre wide, only big enough for one person at a time. Jack hopped across to it, then skipped to another larger stone, hovering a bit higher. Ruby followed, then Danny. The stone he'd leapt from began to rise, as if cushioned by an air current. At the same time, the one they were on sank slightly.

As if starting some chain reaction, all of the stones started to move slowly — some up and down, others side to side.

"Uh-oh — looks like we've upset the balance somehow!" said Ruby.

Jack waited until the one in front passed in range, then stepped onto it. It was like being in a giant rocky computer game. *Only if you fall here, you don't get another life!*

A mighty grinding crash sounded from above as two enormous rocks collided. Stone dust and fragments rained down, and the larger of the two rocks tipped and descended like a sinking ship. Jack jumped forward to the next moving stone.

"Quickly!" he called to the others. "The stones are going to smash themselves to pieces!"

Ruby launched herself onto his rock, but the space was widening too fast, and Danny missed his chance. Jack watched helplessly as his friend drifted downwards and away.

"The rope!" Ruby said.

She took it from Jack and twirled it once around her head before hurling it to Danny who grabbed the end, just in time. The rope went tight, then Jack felt strength flow through his hand. A moment later, Danny's feet left his rock as he dangled below.

"Pull me up!" called Danny.

Jack began to haul up his friend.

Below, Danny's eyes widened in fear. "Watch out!"

Jack looked around just in time to see another floating boulder smash into the rock they were standing on. It juddered beneath their feet. Jack almost lost the grip on the rope, stumbling forward. With a cry, Ruby's foot slipped. Arms wheeling, she toppled backwards off the floating rock.

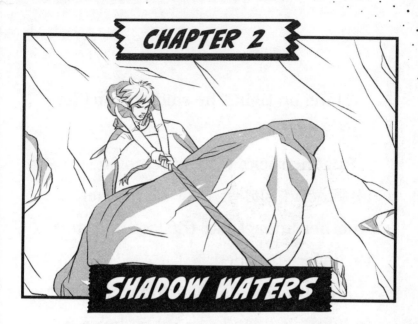

CHAPTER 2

SHADOW WATERS

JACK HEAVED on the rope, swinging Danny like a pendulum in Ruby's direction.

"Grab on!" he shouted to his friend as she plunged.

He felt more than saw Ruby collide with first the rope, and then with Danny, who managed to grab hold of her.

"Hang on tight!" he said. "I won't let you fall!"

But the rocks were still moving all around, sliding past each other. Another impact like the last one, and they were finished.

Jack braced his legs, and was about to haul his friends up, when he saw the rope fraying where it rubbed against the sharp side of the stone. With every heave, it would split more. Jack couldn't take that chance.

"My sensors are picking up elevated heart rate," said Hawk calmly. "Is everything all right, Jack?"

"Not really!" said Jack.

The far edge of the ravine was still ten metres away.

Ah! That's it! Jack realised.

He moved his hands from side to side, trusting his super strength. Below, the rope swayed.

"What are you doing?" cried Ruby, as she swung from side to side.

More rope fibres began to split, until only a few were left.

"I'm going to swing you across!" he called down. Yet more fibres pinged free.

With a great heave, Jack dragged the rope sideways.

"I don't think that's a good

ideaaaaa!" shouted Danny. The rope snapped. Jack fell onto his chest as Danny and Ruby flew through the air. His friends slammed into the lip of the ravine, legs scrambling on the cliff edge. They both managed to pull themselves up.

Jack climbed to his feet. Relief flooded through him, but it didn't last long. He was still too far from the edge of the chasm to jump, and all he had left was a short length of frayed rope. He stumbled as the floating boulder he was standing on collided with a smaller one.

"Look out!" yelled Ruby, pointing

above him. Jack felt a shadow pass over his head. A huge, flat boulder, far bigger than the one he stood on, was dropping right towards him.

"Jack, you have to jump!" said Danny urgently.

"By my calculations, that would be unwise," said Hawk. "You would have to break the world long jump record to make it to the other side."

"Have you got any better ideas?" asked Jack.

Hawk was silent for two or three seconds, before answering, "Not one that ends with you alive."

Jack growled in frustration. He had

ten seconds at most before the large boulder hit. *This is it. I'm going to die.* Then he saw a chance. A small floating stone, barely bigger than a tennis ball, was shooting on a diagonal upward course between him and his friends. There was no time to think. He ran to the edge and jumped into emptiness, hearing his friends shout with fear. His foot found the stone and he pushed, off, slipping at the same time. Stretching desperately, he reached with his hands and closed his eyes.

Thump!

He hit the lip of the ravine, and clung on, his fingers scrabbling for holds.

Hands fastened over his wrists, and Danny said from above. "You're crazy, you know that?"

Jack's friends hauled him up. "I've never been so happy to stand on solid ground," he said. He looked back at the destruction happening over the ravine. Soon there wouldn't be any floating stones left at all. *How will we get home?*

They pressed on. The passage narrowed as barbed metal vines grew thick on the walls and ceiling. These ones seemed more aggressive, straining to snatch at anyone who passed. Jack drew his glowing sword, hacking at them fiercely. Even with the cool suits, the air was stiflingly hot on his head and neck. Soon, Jack was dripping with sweat, and took a moment to rest. His neck prickled as distant chanting drifted through the hot, dark tunnel.

"Can you hear that?" he said. The other two paused to listen. "I think it's Smarm."

"Great!" said Danny. "Even your ears are better than mine now!"

Jack charged forward, swiping away vines with ferocious sweeps of his blade. Suddenly, the passageway opened onto a ledge above an enormous cavern. Below spread a lake. But it wasn't filled with water. Thick currents of shadow writhed over each other like a sea of vipers. It stretched into the darkness, and Jack couldn't see the far shore.

"That's got to be the source of the

poison," said Jack. Chanting echoed
off the cavern walls, a constant
stream of strange words.

"Where's Smarm?" said Ruby.

"I can't see him," Jack replied.
Ahead, the ledge dropped away into a
steep slope. "Be careful," he muttered,

as he began to scramble down,
slipping on loose scree.

Ruby zoomed past him, riding her
shield like it was a snowboard. Danny
was the last to reach the bottom. He
stared fearfully at the lake of shadow.

"I think the chanting is coming from
this way," Jack said. He led them
along the edge of the cavern, staying
a good distance from the banks of
the shadow lake. The air above it
shimmered like a heat haze, and Jack
thought he could hear it whispering.
He wondered what would happen if
he were to fall in. Chosen One or not,
he didn't want to find out.

The chanting became louder. The ruins of ancient buildings appeared along the shore. There were no statues, but there were shattered, toppled columns, and tumbled archways of stone.

"Hey, look at this," said Ruby, from the top of a crumbling set of stairs.

Jack and Danny joined her. It was a nest of some sort. The eggs were almost as tall as Jack's waist, purple and dotted with silver streaks. Others had already hatched and were empty shells.

"I wonder what creature has laid these," said Danny.

One of the eggs wobbled, and from beneath the shell a light grew bright.

"I think we're about to find out," said Jack, stepping back.

Crack.

The egg fell sideways and a black shape burst from the side, along with a trail of smoke.

Then flames took hold, and the egg shell came apart completely. A little flame lizard flopped out, uncoiling its long tail.

"Of course! They're

Tartania's eggs!" said Ruby.

The baby lizard shook some loose shell from its head, then turned to them with a chirruping sound.

"I guess that's why she's so angry!" said Jack. "Bulk and Smarm have blocked her from her nest with those metallic vines."

"Ah, you've arrived just in time," said a familiar voice.

Jack and his friends spun round. From a ruined corridor above, Bulk and his skeleton force descended. There were only six now, and one was missing an arm. Bulk's tunic was torn, and his face was grazed.

Jack pointed Blaze. "Stay back!" he said.

"You won't catch us off guard this time. Prepare to attack!" The skeletons raised their bone blades. "Come quietly and we won't hurt you," Bulk said to Jack.

Danny drew out his crossbow, loading a bolt. "No chance."

"I was hoping you'd say that." Bulk grinned and raised his sword. "Attack!" he roared.

CHAPTER 3

GENERAL GORE'S RETURN

THE BABY flame lizard scampered away as the skeletons charged. One warrior exploded as Danny's bolt struck its chest, and Jack cleaved another in two with his sword. Its body toppled to the ground, but its legs continued running a few steps before falling too. Bulk swung a heavy mace on a chain around his head and Jack ducked as it whipped towards him.

He heard Ruby cry out as two skeletons gripped her arms. Danny aimed his crossbow at them, but to fire would risk hitting Ruby.

Jack ducked Bulk's mace once again. But this time he stumbled back and tripped as the top half of the fallen skeleton warrior gripped his ankle. Two more bone creatures dived on him, each holding one of his arms. Bulk approached, swinging the mace in a wide arc, the steel ball sweeping

in a vicious downward strike towards
his head. There wasn't time to move.
Jack threw off a skeleton then held up
a hand and caught the lump of metal
in his scaled, glowing fingers. Bulk's
eyes went wide as Jack crushed it into
fragments.

Jack jumped up when he felt a
sword against his throat. The skeleton
holding it grinned toothily at him.

Ruby was still being restrained and
Danny was surrounded.

"Take their weapons," said Bulk.

Jack glowered at Bulk, but he had
no choice. He passed his blade to a
skeleton, who snatched it from him.

"I told you not to fight," said Bulk. He gave Jack a vicious kick to the chest. Pain exploded down Jack's flank, causing his vision to flare white. He rolled over, willing the agony to stop.

"Coward!" Ruby shouted at Bulk.

"Shut your mouth," said Bulk. "If I had my way, we'd kill you all. Tie these so-called heroes up," he ordered his soldiers.

Jack saw one of Danny's crossbow bolts on the floor among the remains of a skeleton soldier. He slipped it up his sleeve without anyone seeing, then let himself be hoisted up and bound with ropes, arms pinned to his side so that he wouldn't be able to use his super-strong hands to help him escape.

"What have you done with Ms Steel?" snapped Danny.

"Funny you should ask that," said Bulk nastily. "We were just about to take you to her."

He began to march away along the banks of the lake. A skeleton gave Jack a shove and they followed.

"This is all my fault," muttered Danny to the others. "I should have heard him coming."

"Don't be silly," said Ruby. "The shadow's sapped your power."

I'm the only one still with my abilities, thought Jack. *My friends need me more than ever.*

Smarm's chanting grew louder as they skirted the black water. Jack spotted more knotted metallic vines growing across several openings in the wall, their roots reaching back to the lake, as if they'd grown right out of the shadows.

The lake must be the source of the vines' power.

Through the gloom Jack saw a barred cage hanging from a chain over the surface of the lake. A figure was slumped inside. A head lifted weakly, and Jack saw a shock of purple hair.

"Ms Steel!" cried Ruby, struggling against her bonds.

Ms Steel shuffled and gripped the

bars. "No!" she said weakly. "You shouldn't be here."

From beneath the lake's surface, bubbles and tongues of shadow whipped thirstily towards the cage, causing Ms Steel to slump weakly to the cage floor.

"We'll get you out!" said Jack. A short gangway reached from the shore to the cage.

Smarm stepped forward in his brown robes to greet Bulk. The tall, thin sorcerer towered over his comrade. He was clutching General Gore's black helmet.

"Brought you a little gift," said Bulk,

nodding towards Jack and his friends.

"Excellent," hissed Smarm. Jack saw his pointed tongue flickering between the black shards of his teeth. "They're here just in time to witness the ... reawakening."

He lifted General Gore's helmet, chanting again, and shadows poured from the mouth-guard and visor into the lake below, a torrent of black poison. The lake spat and seethed like something alive, and a voice filled the air, so soft that Jack wondered if he was imagining it.

I am coming. I grow strong. The Age of Noxx is upon us.

"We await you, Master!" cried Smarm. He let go of the helmet, but instead of falling to the ground, it floated across the surface of the lake, then descended.

"How is that possible?" Jack breathed, staring in utter horror as the shadow waters reached up their snaking tendrils and seized the helmet, pulling it beneath the surface soundlessly. "I saw Gore die ..." *I need to stop this!*

With all eyes fixed on the spot where the helmet had submerged, Jack let the bolt he'd hidden slide from his sleeve. He began to work the

tip against the ropes that bound
him. He had to be careful not to slip
and cut himself.

"Er ... now what?" said Bulk,
breaking the silence.

"Now we wait, you imbecile," said
Smarm impatiently.

Jack felt his ropes loosening. Ruby
and Danny had both noticed what
he was doing.

"Maybe it hasn't worked," said Bulk
after a few more seconds.

"Just watch the prisoners," said
Smarm angrily. "Leave the important
stuff to me."

As Bulk turned his attention to

them, Danny threw himself forward in front of Jack and shouted, "You won't get away with this!"

He's trying to give me time, Jack thought.

The skeletons quickly grabbed Danny again.

"You're too late, I'm afraid," said Smarm slyly. "Our plan has worked to perfection. This place is steeped in magic — it's been a Noxxian temple for ten thousand years. We had to clear the lizard infestation from the mountain, and keep them out with the shadow-weed. But the most important part of the plan was finding a new body for our master's spirit. That's where the unfortunate Ms Steel comes in."

Jack was horrified. So that was why Ms Steel was in the cage! He focused on working the arrowhead on the ropes that bound his arms. A skeleton a few paces to his left was clutching Blaze, which glowed brightly in protest. But the warrior was watching the lake as well.

"Look!" cried Bulk, pointing a stubby, dirt-caked finger.

Jack and the others stared as something broke the surface of the lake. It was the helmet. But as it rose,

a form appeared beneath it, a twisted
wraith-like figure made of swirling
shadow. It had the unmistakable
shape of General Gore.

"Master!" hissed Smarm, falling to
his knees.

Jack watched as the shadow man glided across the lake's surface towards Ms Steel's cage. Inside, she pressed herself back against the bars, unable to get away.

"Take her body!" said Smarm. "Become whole once more!"

No chance! thought Jack. With a final slice, the ropes around his wrists fell away. He ran and drove a fist into the chest of the skeleton holding his sword. It exploded, and Jack caught the hilt.

Danny and Ruby struggled against their ropes.

"Grab him!" said Bulk.

Jack ran again, not at Bulk or Smarm, or the skeletons, or to free his friends, but towards the cavern.

"Running away!" Bulk laughed. "Not such a hero now, is he?"

Guess again, Jack thought. The vines reached for his neck and arms, but he slashed at the knotted roots as hard as he could, slicing straight through them. Severed from the shadow-lake, they withered at once, blackening and crumbling away before his eyes.

I hope this works.

Jack turned to see the remaining skeletons advancing towards him.

As he raised Blaze to defend himself, he heard the patter and scrape of clawed feet. He looked over his shoulder. A red glow filled the tunnel. The skeletons all stopped, looking at each other.

"What are you waiting for?" asked Bulk. "Kill the boy!"

A burst of flame licked through the tunnel — then Tartania's huge rocky head appeared. Her crimson eyes blazed. Jack had never been so happy to see a giant flame lizard. He pointed his blade at the skeletons.

"They drove you from your home, poisoned your land and kept you from your babies," he cried. "Take back what is yours, Tartania!"

Her eyes turned on the Noxxian warriors. She opened her cavernous mouth, flames licking around her huge teeth. She let out a deafening roar that shook Jack's body.

Then she charged.

CHAPTER 4

TARTANIA'S REVENGE

JACK DIVED aside. The massive flame lizard smashed into the skeletons like skittles. He watched in awe as they were reduced to flying bones. A skull bounced in front of his feet, its mouth still open in shock.

Tartania barrelled down towards the lake, making the cavern floor tremble.

Wreaths of fire spurted from her huge rocky mouth, burning the remaining vines to dust. Jack heard more trampling and, a second later, her dozens of children raced into the cave from the cleared entrances, shrieking madly. Bulk dropped his mace and bounded away, leaving Smarm to face the pack of flame lizards, orbs of magic glowing round his hands. His eyes flicked to the shadow lake. The dark shape of General Gore reached out his hands and gripped hold of the cage, then hoisted himself towards Ms Steel.

A stab of fear jolted down Jack's

spine. He set off, jumping over broken bones and rocks and scattered fires towards the gangplank.

General Gore turned towards Jack when he reached the cage. There was no face inside his helmet, only black shadow.

You will not stop me! rasped a voice like the howl of wind.

"I won't let you take over Ms Steel!" Jack cried. He drew back Blaze. The shadow figure covered his eyes against the glare of the shining blade. Jack plunged his sword into the general's writhing body. With a hissing cry, Gore released the bars

and dropped back into the lake.
The shadows swirled and splashed
around them angrily.

Jack sheathed the sword. Crumpled
against the side of the cage, Ms Steel
flickered her eyes open.

"I'll get you out!" Jack said. He

gripped two of the bars and pulled. The steel groaned and with a roar of effort, Jack snapped them off. He reached out a hand. "Trust me."

"I do," Ms Steel croaked, gripping hold of Jack's scaled wrist.

Jack pulled her free of the cage as his friends rushed over to the edge of the gangplank. Jack's heart swelled with relief that they were all safe.

On the banks, Smarm was hurling balls of energy from his hands, trying to keep the flame lizards at bay. Bulk was nowhere to be seen.

That was when Jack realised the water of the shadow lake was changing. The shadows were splitting apart like shredding mist. From beneath came the dazzling glow of pure turquoise.

Gore's poison is fading ...

With a cry of alarm, Smarm rushed to the water's edge, wading into the shallows. "Master!"

Jack saw him scooping through the remains of the shadow. The flame lizards on the bank didn't dare to follow all the way to the water's edge, but blew spurts of fire in the sorcerer's direction. Smarm staggered onto the far bank, cloak on fire, and ran off towards one of the openings in the cavern wall. Tartania and her brood were close behind.

Ms Steel stood unsteadily. "Thank you," she said.

"You came to help us in Noxx," Jack said. "We couldn't leave you here."

Danny's head raised up and he grinned. "I can hear properly again!"

"That's because the shadows have retreated," said Ms Steel.

Jack looked across the deserted cavern, wondering if Smarm and Bulk had managed to get away, or if Tartania had caught up and taken her revenge. He didn't really care — the main thing was that his friends were safe and General Gore was defeated.

"Wait! What's that?" said Ruby.

She pointed at the lake and Jack saw something bobbing on the surface towards them.

"General Gore's helmet," Jack said. He reached out across the water and grabbed it. The thick plates of jet black metal were cold to the touch and made his skin crawl.

"What do you think we should do with it?" asked Danny.

Jack placed the helmet at his feet, then drew his sword. No one tried to stop him or said anything at all as

he brought the sunsteel blade down.
Sparks flew off as the helmet broke
into two down the middle.

CHAPTER 5

A FINAL PERIL

"WELL, LET'S hope that's the last we see of him," said Ms Steel. Her legs wobbled a little, and they all rushed to support her.

"Hang on," said Danny, suddenly alert. "I hear something."

Jack felt the ground tremble a little under his feet. Looking down, he realised it was the pieces of the helmet. A few trickles of shadow were still pooling around it, and the sections themselves were vibrating.

"Are you sure he's gone?" asked Danny. "For good, this time?"

"I don't know," said Ms Steel.

The air hummed with energy, and the cracks began to appear across the helmet fragments.

"I think it's going to explode," said Ruby fearfully.

A voice whispered from the helmet. *That's right, girl. And you are all going to die!*

Jack grabbed the pieces, shadows

licking over his fingers, and hurled them into the middle of the lake. They landed with a splosh and sank away into the depths.

"That was close!" said Danny. "For a second I thought—"

BOOM!

The lake's surface erupted, throwing gallons and gallons of water into the air. Jack froze as a tidal wave a hundred feet tall rolled towards them. There was nothing they could do.

We're going to be swallowed …

He felt an arm crush him close.

"Get next to me!" cried Ms Steel as she also grabbed Ruby and Danny.

She closed her eyes. The mountain
of water swept over them in a
deafening rush and Jack closed his
eyes too. His body was picked up like
a rag doll. Icy water streamed into his
mouth and nose.

For a second, he thought he
saw a glowing purple light. He felt
weightless, like he was surrounded by
air rather than water. Suddenly the
roar of the water was gone.

And when Jack opened his eyes,
he found himself on his back
looking at blue sky. Ruby and Danny
clutched each other beside him,
completely drenched.

"We're not dead," Jack gurgled.

"Aren't we?" asked Danny, hair
plastered over his face.

"We're at the academy!" said Ruby,
jumping up.

Jack pushed himself onto his

elbows and saw she was right. The walls of the ancient fort rose above them, the flags of the school flying across the battlements. They were lying in the main courtyard.

But where's—?

"Ms Steel!" cried Ruby.

Jack's heart skipped a beat as he saw their teacher lying a few metres away on her side.

She was not moving.

"Quick!" he said. "We need to get her to the infirmary!"

• • •

Two hours later, they stood beside Ms Steel's bed with Chancellor Rex.

The headmaster looked grave as the monitors beeped softly.

"Will she be all right?" asked Jack.

"Only time will tell," said the chancellor. "We cannot identify the cause of her coma, but we think it has something to do with her prolonged exposure to the shadow."

They'd explained as much as they could to the chancellor, but no one knew for sure what Ms Steel had suffered before they had rescued her from the cage. Smarm might have tortured her, or perhaps the proximity of Gore's spirit had managed to infect her somehow.

A more worrying thought occurred to Jack. "Could it be because she teleported us with her?" he said. "Maybe it was too much for her body to handle."

"Perhaps," said the chancellor. "She had never done it before, as far as

I'm aware. But you cannot blame yourselves. Ms Steel wouldn't be here at all if it weren't for you three."

Through the windows of the infirmary, Jack saw the battlements thronging with students in their uniforms. Gradually, Hero Academy was returning to normal, with all the search parties returning from their outposts.

Professor Rufus entered the room. "Has there been any change?" he asked, his voice full of concern.

"No," said Jack. He felt wracked with guilt. *What if Ms Steel never wakes up?*

Professor Rufus took a heavy breath. "We've completed our analysis of the underground cavern," he said. "There are no signs of further Noxxian activity. It looks like the temple has been abandoned for good this time."

"Tartania has her home back," said Ruby, smiling.

"Thank you, professor," said Chancellor Rex. "Please do one more sweep, just to be sure."

After Professor Rufus left, Jack spoke quietly to Chancellor Rex.

"You think General Gore's coming back again, don't you?" he said.

"I honestly don't know," said the headmaster, "but I don't want to take any chances. Our enemies will not rest — so we mustn't, either."

He left the bedside and walked in front of one of the monitors, which was linked directly to Ms Steel's brainwaves.

"Few people know this, but Ms Steel is a bit ... different," he said.

"Well, we're all a bit different, aren't we?" said Ruby. "That's why we're all here at Hero Academy in the first place."

"Ms Steel is special, even among Team Hero," the chancellor said.

"Some of us have powers that come from different places."

"What does that mean?" Jack asked.

"What it might mean," the chancellor continued, "is that there could be another way to cure her."

His eyes flashed.

Jack stepped closer to the bed.

"We'll do whatever it takes ..."

THE END

TIMETABLE

	MON	TUE	WED	THUR	FRI
08.00	ASSEMBLY	ASSEMBLY	ASSEMBLY	ASSEMBLY	ASSEMBLY
09.00	POWERS	POWERS	POWERS	POWERS	POWERS
10.00	COMBAT	STRATEGY	TECH	COMBAT	STRATEGY
11.00	MATHS	GEOGRAPHY	ENGLISH	HISTORY	ENGLISH
12.00	HISTORY	SCIENCE	MATHS	SCIENCE	GEOGRAPHY
13.00	LUNCH!				
14.00	TECH	COMBAT	COMBAT	STRATEGY	WEAPON TRAINING
15.00	GYM	GYM	WEAPON TRAINING	GYM	GYM
16.00	GYM	GYM	GYM	GYM	HOMEWORK
17.00	HOMEWORK	HOMEWORK	HOMEWORK	HOMEWORK	FREE

...ARRIORS HAD SPECIAL POWERS, AND
...NEW EACH OTHER WELL – THEY MET ONCE
...YEAR AT A SECRET TOURNAMENT TO
...RACTISE THEIR FIGHTING SKILLS. EACH

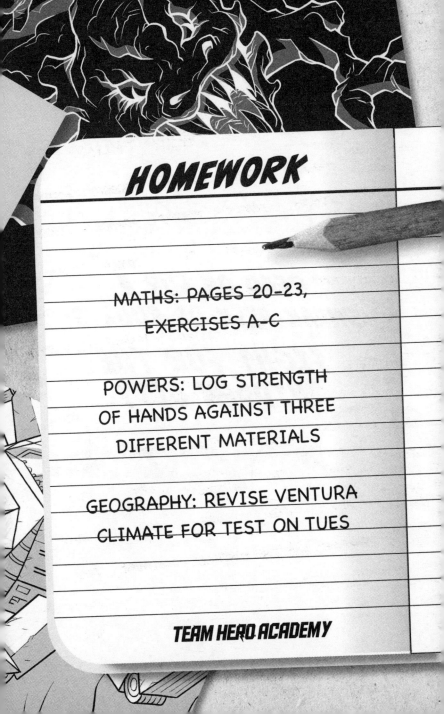

CHAPTER 1

DESTINATION: KHALEA

The jet plane knifed through the sky at close to the speed of sound, but Jack barely felt any movement where he sat.

"This is so cool!" said Danny excitedly, sitting beside him. He tucked back his hair to reveal over-sized, bat-like ears. "The engines are so quiet, even I can barely hear them!"

The students were seated in the back of Arrow, the Hero Academy aircraft. They faced each other in two rows. Jack sat between Danny and Ruby, his best friends at the school. Opposite, an older boy called Olly was with his gang, taking it in turns to scowl or snigger.

"Hey, snake-hands!" said Olly.

For a moment, Jack felt like he was back at his old school in Ventura City. He'd spent years thinking that the strange scaly skin on his hands made him a freak, but he'd recently discovered that they possessed incredible strength. That's why he

was now a student at Hero Academy
— a secret school for the gifted. Every
student had a different power. All of
them were training to become part of
Team Hero, the ancient organisation
that protected earth from the evil of
the realms at the centre of the earth.

"You think you'll survive
Flammara?" said Olly. "It's pretty
brutal down there. Over forty
degrees in the daytime, below
freezing at night."

"We'll manage, thanks," said Jack.
"You just look after yourself."

Olly's smirk vanished. "You think
you're special, don't you? Just

because Chancellor Rex thinks you're the so-called Chosen One!"

"Ignore him," muttered Ruby, her striking orange eyes flashing. "He's just jealous."

Chancellor Rex believed Jack was the answer to an ancient prophecy — the Chosen One who would save the human world from the forces of shadow. The headmaster was even more convinced of this after Jack had defeated the evil General Gore in a one-on-one duel in the underground kingdom of Noxx itself. Jack and his friends had also destroyed Gore's armies of shadow warriors before they could swarm the Earth's surface. Jack had gone from being a zero at his old school in Ventura City, looked down on by everyone, to the saviour of the human race. But deep down, Jack still felt like a normal boy. Sometimes he wondered if he was in some weird dream.

Check out book 5:
FIGHT FOR THE HIDDEN CITY
to find out what happens next!

FREE TEAM HERO CLUB PACK

IN EVERY BOOK OF TEAM HERO SERIES ONE there is a special Power Token. Collect all four tokens to get an exclusive Team Hero Club pack. The pack contains everything you and your friends need to form your very own Team Hero Club.

MEMBERSHIP CARDS · MEMBERSHIP CERTIFICATE · STICKERS · POWER GAME · BOOKMARKS

Just fill in the form below, send it in with your four tokens and we'll send you your Team Hero Club Pack.

SEND TO: Team Hero Club Pack Offer, Hachette Children's Books, Marketing Department, Carmelite House, 50 Victoria Embankment, London, EC4Y 0DZ.

CLOSING DATE: 31st December 2017

WWW.TEAMHEROBOOKS.CO.UK

Please complete using capital letters *(UK and republic of Ireland residents only)*

FIRST NAME

SURNAME

DATE OF BIRTH

ADDRESS LINE 1

ADDRESS LINE 2

ADDRESS LINE 3

POSTCODE

PARENT OR GUARDIAN'S EMAIL

☐ I'd like to receive Team Hero email newsletters and information about other great Hachette Children's Group offers (I can unsubscribe at any time)

Terms and conditions apply. For full terms and conditions please go to teamherobooks.co.uk/terms

TEAM HERO TOKEN

TEAM HERO Club packs available while stocks last. Terms and conditions apply